The Cafeteria Contest

by Mary Bendix
illustrated by David Lowe

 HOUGHTON MIFFLIN HARCOURT
School Publishers

Copyright © by Houghton Mifflin Harcourt Publishing Company

Printed in China

ISBN-13: 978-0-547-02512-4
ISBN-10: 0-547-02512-2

13 14 15 16 0940 19 18 17 16
4500569761

Louisa Hill, the cook at Woodlake School's cafeteria, was going to retire. Everyone wanted to do something special for her. Mr. Graves, the principal, decided to hold a contest. Each fifth-grade class would make a tasty dish. Mrs. Hill would sample each one and choose a winner. The winning dish would be named in her honor.

Ms. Silverman's class decided to cook a classic recipe. On the day of the contest, they were excited. Their casserole was bubbling away in the oven.

Elisa, Tad, and Quentin watch their casserole cook in the oven.

The forgotten cans of tuna

"Mrs. Hill will love our dish!" said Tad, cleaning off the counter. "Wait a second. What's this?" He pulled a stack of cans from behind the blender. The cans wobbled and fell, rolling in every direction.

Quentin picked up a can. "Oh, no, it's the tuna! We forgot to put tuna in the tuna noodle casserole!"

Elisa looked horrified. Then she started laughing. "So, what's cooking?" she asked.

"I haven't got a clue," said Tad, "but it smells delicious!"

Quentin double-checked the ingredients list. "We didn't leave out anything else. Let's just forget the tuna and hope it tastes as good as it smells."

Amy and Sophia stir the sauce.

Meanwhile, Mrs. Trang's class was cooking, too. Sophia and Amy stirred sauce while they waited for Alexi to arrive with the ziti.

"Keep stirring," said Sophia. She handed the spoon to Amy. "I'll fill the big pot with water and put it on to boil. It will be ready to go when Alexi gets here with the..."

Just then Alexi burst through the doors and interrupted Sophia in the middle of her sentence. "Never fear, I'm here!" he said, swinging his bag up onto the counter.

Sophia looked at the bag. "What in the world are those?"

"Ziti," said Alexi. He popped a cherry tomato into his mouth.

"Alexi, this isn't *ziti*. It's *zucchini!*" said Sophia, holding up a green vegetable.

Alexi frowned. "Isn't that the same thing? Don't you call zucchini *ziti* for short?"

"No," said Amy. She struggled to hold her temper. "Ziti is like macaroni, only bigger—and it's shaped like a tube. This isn't pasta, Alexi. It's *squash!*"

"We're just going to have to use zucchini instead of ziti," said Sophia. "Let's cook it and cover it with our yummy tomato sauce."

"Will that work?" asked Amy.

"Absolutely," said Sophia. "My grandmother substitutes stuff like this all the time. This sauce is good on anything. It will taste great."

Zucchini, not ziti!

Mr. Trueblood's class was busy making a specialty worthy of their favorite cook.

"I love Mrs. Hill," said Chima sadly. "I can't believe that she's leaving. No one makes Friday Surprise like she does."

"Slow down," said Diego. "You've grated enough cheese. You'll bury the macaroni!"

"Is the macaroni supposed to be this crunchy? Mrs. Hill's is usually softer," said Rob.

"Mrs. Hill's is perfect," said Chima. "Our's can never be that good."

Rob, Chima, and Diego make macaroni and cheese.

Ready to be judged

At lunchtime, students crowded into the cafeteria. Sophia, Chima, and Quentin staggered in. Each of them carried a big pan covered with foil. They set the pans on the counter, bumping and jostling each other.

"You're squishing me!" said Sophia to Chima.

"Move over!" said Chima to Quentin.

"I need some room here!" said Quentin to no one in particular.

"Settle down, everyone," said Mrs. Trang. "Here comes the guest of honor."

Principal Graves brought Mrs. Hill into the cafeteria. Everyone clapped.

Principal Graves thanks Louisa Hill for her wonderful cooking.

Principal Graves gave a speech. "Mrs. Hill, we want to thank you for many years of wonderful food. I personally want to thank you for your chicken noodle soup. I've eaten it every week for 16 years and enjoyed every drop."

Louisa Hill beamed.

"Now it's time for you to judge our contest," said Mr. Graves. "The fifth graders have been hard at work, developing recipes to honor your years of service. We'd like you to do a taste test. Please try each dish and pick a winner."

Mrs. Hill leaned over the first pan. She closed her eyes and took a long sniff.

"Oh, doesn't this smell fine," she said.

She lifted a forkful up to her mouth and nodded as she chewed. A smile spread across her face.

The kids watched as she smelled the second dish and lifted a nice big bite up to her lips. She chewed thoughtfully for a minute and then murmured, "Oh, yes indeed."

Time to judge the contest

The kids didn't take their eyes off Mrs. Hill as she tasted the last dish. They thought she would announce a winner right away, but she didn't. She stood for a moment with her fork in midair and then she tried all three dishes again. At last, she set her fork down and dabbed her mouth with a napkin.

"Well, you children have certainly been creative in making these dishes. For instance, this casserole is very light." Quentin caught Elisa's eye. "It might be good with a little tuna thrown in. Still, that extra lumpiness could detract from the smooth, creamy sauce."

Quentin and Elisa listen to Mrs. Hill.

Mrs. Hill talks about the dish with zucchini.

Mrs. Hill pointed to the second pan. "This casserole is quite nice, too. One might expect a starchy pasta to be holding it up. Instead, there is a base of sweet zucchini under a tangy tomato sauce. Most kids won't eat anything green, I'm here to tell you—but none of you would pass up *this* magnificent dish. It might benefit from a little cheese on top, but it stands alone just fine."

Sophia winked at Amy and Alexi.

Mrs. Hill moved to the third pan. "Now, this third dish is hard to mess up. You can undercook it, you can overcook it, you can run out of cheese, you can load it on, and you can burn it to a crisp. No matter what you do, children the world over will beg for more. It has always been one of my favorites because it's so forgiving. It's always made with great affection and high hopes. I know the children who made this dish had hearts just filled with love. I feel it. I really do."

Rob and Diego smiled at Chima.

Diego, Rob, and Chima are happy with their dish.

Louisa Hill creates a winning dish.

Mrs. Hill reached under the counter. She pulled out a large serving spoon and a clean plate. "If you ask me, all of these dishes are winners," she said. As she spoke, Mrs. Hill loaded up the plate. "But all of them could be better. If you were to take a little of this noodle casserole, add a layer of zucchini with tomato sauce, and top the whole thing off with cheese, I think you'd be hard put to find a tastier meal!"

That is how the prize-winning dish was invented. Principal Graves still misses Mrs. Hill's soup, and everyone still misses Mrs. Hill. They remember her every Friday at lunch, though. That's when they get to eat a tasty plate of *Mrs. Hill's Choice.*

The Friday favorite is *Mrs. Hill's Choice.*

Responding

✔ **TARGET SKILL** **Story Structure** What problem must be solved in *The Cafeteria Contest*? What are the important events? What is the solution? Copy and complete the diagram below.

Problem	Events
Louisa Hill, the cook, must choose a winner from among dishes made in her honor by the fifth graders.	? ? ?
Solution Louisa mixes together the students' dishes to make a tasty dish called *Mrs. Hill's Choice*.	

Write About It

Text to Self The students in *The Cafeteria Contest* work in teams to cook for Mrs. Hill. Think about a time when you were in a contest as part of a team. Write a paragraph telling what happened.

✔ **TARGET SKILL** **Story Structure** Examine details about characters, setting, and plot.

✔ **TARGET STRATEGY** **Summarize** Briefly tell the important parts of the text in your own words.

GENRE **Humorous Fiction** is a story that is written to entertain the reader.